This **OCTONAUTS** Annual belongs to

....

OCTONAUTS™

ANNUAL 2012

CONTENTS

EGMONT

First published in Great Britain in 2011
by Egmont UK Limited, 239 Kensington High Street, London W8 6SA

Written by Leah James, Jude Exley, Laura Green and Jane Riordan.
Designed by Catherine Ellis.
Special thanks to Kathy and Amy Turner for the GUP-A craft activity.

OCTONAUTS™ OCTOPOD™ Copyright © 2011 Chorion Rights Limited. All rights reserved.

ISBN 978 1 4052 6102 9
3 5 7 9 10 8 6 4 2
Printed in Italy

CALLING ALL OCTONAUTS!

Hello, Captain Barnacles here! Welcome to the new Octonauts Annual. Your mission is to come on board the Octopod and help the crew to **EXPLORE, RESCUE, PROTECT!**

Colour in the picture of Captain Barnacles as neatly as you can.

Kwazii has hidden some treasure maps in this annual. Can you find them all? Write how many there are in the circle. **OCTONAUTS, LET'S DO THIS!**

LET'S DO THIS!

Come and meet The Octonauts – a team of undersea adventurers who are always ready to dive into action!

01 CAPTAIN BARNACLES

NAME: Captain Barnacles Bear

JOB: Leader of the Octonauts

OCTO-FACT: Barnacles is strong enough to lift a giant clam!

GEAR: Octo-Compass, binoculars

SAYS: "Sound the Octo-Alert!"

02 KWAZII

NAME: Lieutenant Kwazii Cat

JOB: Second in command to Captain Barnacles

OCTO-FACT: Kwazii loves racing dolphins in GUP-B

GEAR: Treasure chest, spyglass

SAYS: "Shiver me whiskers!"

PESO

03

NAME: Medic Peso Penguin

JOB: Helping any creature who is hurt or sick

OCTO-FACT: Peso is the youngest member of the crew

GEAR: Bandage, medical kit

SAYS: "Flappity flippers!"

TWEAK

04

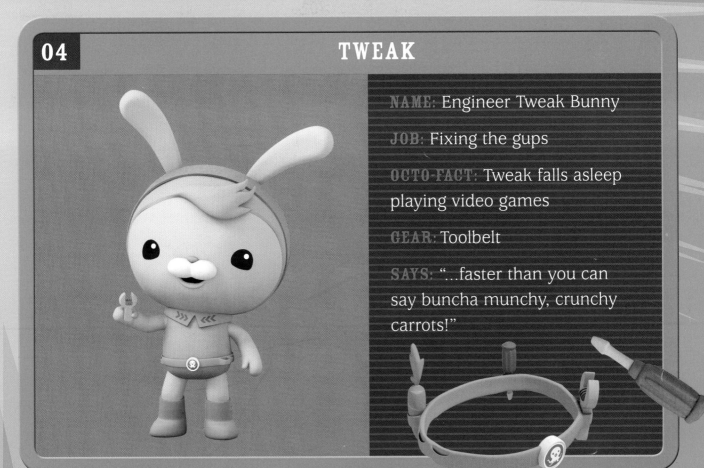

NAME: Engineer Tweak Bunny

JOB: Fixing the gups

OCTO-FACT: Tweak falls asleep playing video games

GEAR: Toolbelt

SAYS: "...faster than you can say buncha munchy, crunchy carrots!"

05 DASHI

NAME: Dashi Dog

JOB: Photographer and computer expert

OCTO-FACT: Dashi has taken photos inside the belly of a whale shark!

GEAR: Camera

SAYS: "Say Seaweed!"

06 SHELLINGTON

NAME: Shellington Sea Otter

JOB: Field researcher

OCTO-FACT: Shellington is a terrible driver and the only Octonaut who can speak Vegimalese

GEAR: Waterproof bag, magnifying glass

SAYS: "Jumpin' Jellyfish!"

07 PROFESSOR INKLING

NAME: Professor Inkling Octopus

JOB: Studying the ocean

OCTO-FACT: Professor Inkling is the founder of the Octonauts

GEAR: Hover chair, library books

SAYS: "Fascinating!"

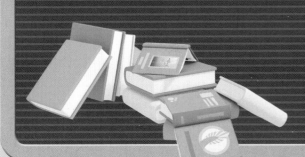

08 TUNIP

NAME: Tunip the Vegimal

JOB: Cook and gardener

OCTO-FACT: Tunip is half tuna, half turnip!

FAVOURITE DISH: Kelp cakes

SAYS: "Chipa, chipa!"

THE SUBMERSIBLES

The Octonauts couldn't dive into action without their extraordinary range of submersibles!

GUP-A

Octonauts' main sub for exploration and travel. Looks like an angler fish.

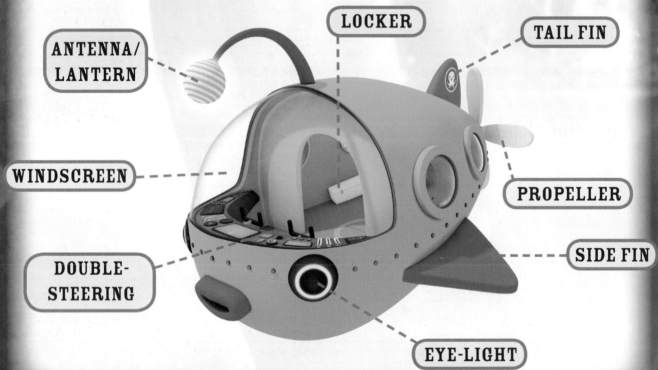

- ANTENNA/LANTERN
- LOCKER
- TAIL FIN
- WINDSCREEN
- PROPELLER
- DOUBLE-STEERING
- SIDE FIN
- EYE-LIGHT

GUP-B

Speedy sub with a "turbo button" for extra speed in an emergency. Looks like a tiger shark.

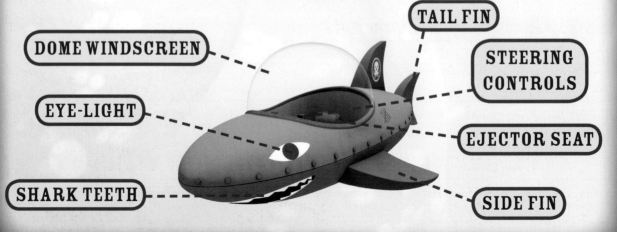

- DOME WINDSCREEN
- TAIL FIN
- STEERING CONTROLS
- EYE-LIGHT
- EJECTOR SEAT
- SHARK TEETH
- SIDE FIN

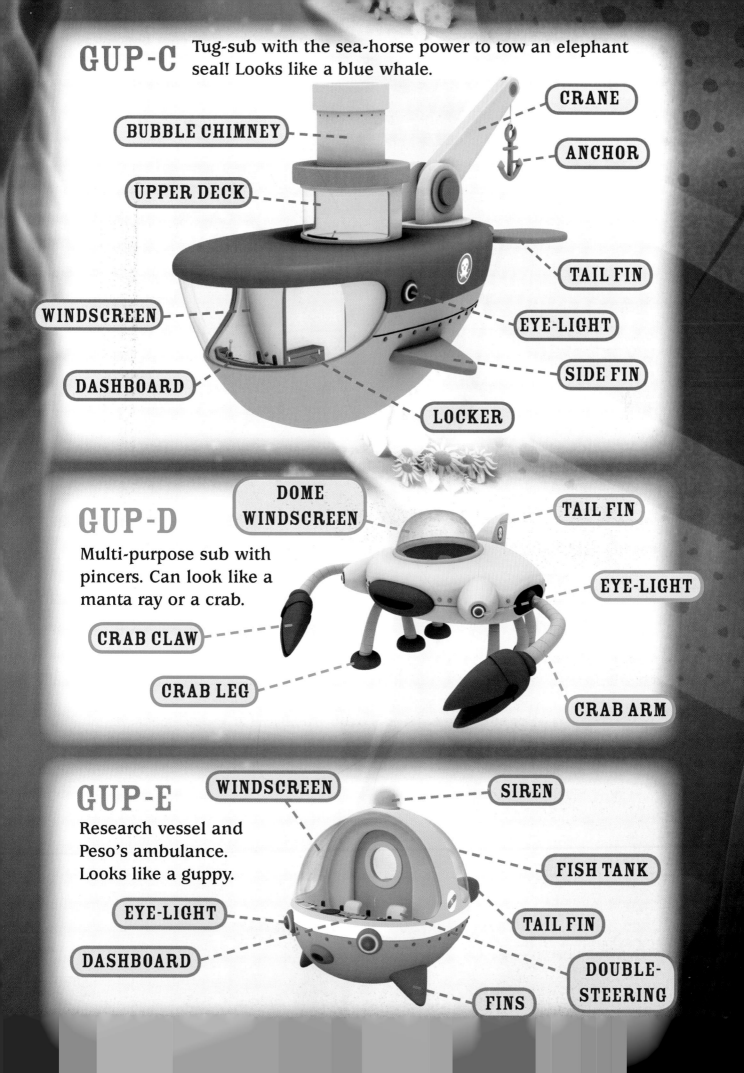

GUP-C Tug-sub with the sea-horse power to tow an elephant seal! Looks like a blue whale.

- CRANE
- ANCHOR
- BUBBLE CHIMNEY
- UPPER DECK
- TAIL FIN
- WINDSCREEN
- EYE-LIGHT
- SIDE FIN
- DASHBOARD
- LOCKER

GUP-D

Multi-purpose sub with pincers. Can look like a manta ray or a crab.

- DOME WINDSCREEN
- TAIL FIN
- EYE-LIGHT
- CRAB CLAW
- CRAB LEG
- CRAB ARM

GUP-E

Research vessel and Peso's ambulance. Looks like a guppy.

- WINDSCREEN
- SIREN
- FISH TANK
- EYE-LIGHT
- TAIL FIN
- DASHBOARD
- DOUBLE-STEERING
- FINS

THE OCTOPOD

Take a closer look at the Octonauts' amazing mobile home base!

KWAZII'S ROOM

MANUAL STEERING WHEEL

GARDEN POD

OCTO-HATCH

OCTONAUTS HQ

GAME POD

LIBRARY

LAUNCH BAY

THE LAB

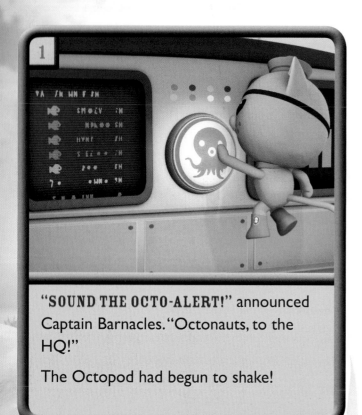

1

"**SOUND THE OCTO-ALERT!**" announced Captain Barnacles. "Octonauts, to the HQ!"

The Octopod had begun to shake!

2

"Whoa!" said Peso. "What was that?"

"That, Peso, was the ocean floor shaking," said Professor Inkling. "Fascinating!"

3

Peso wobbled. The Octopod was tipping!

"Our mission is to get the Octopod standing straight again!" said Captain Barnacles. "**OCTONAUTS, LET'S DO THIS!**"

4

Captain Barnacles, Tweak and Kwazii swam out to see what had made the Octopod tip.

"Aha!" said Captain Barnacles. "The leg is broken!"

5

Tweak jumped into the GUP-D.

"No worries, Cap. I'll have it fixed faster than you can say buncha munchy, crunchy carrots!"

6

While Tweak fixed the Octopod, Kwazii and Barnacles found some squeaking pink slime by a rock.

"Yeow! What's that?" said Kwazii. "It sounds like it's hurt!"

7

"It's a snot sea cucumber!" said the Captain. "She must have been hurt when the ocean floor shook."

"Shiver me whiskers!" said Kwazii. "We need Peso!"

8

Peso jumped into the GUP-E and raced down to Kwazii and Captain Barnacles.

Peso was always ready to help any sick sea creature, no matter what!

9 When Peso arrived, the crew put the snot sea cucumber onto a stretcher and carried her to the GUP-E. There was no time to lose!

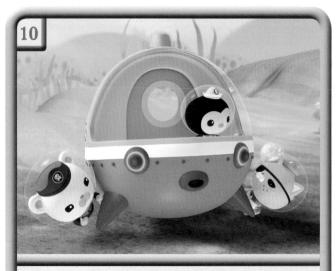

10 Peso launched the GUP-E and raced back to the Octopod at full speed. This was a first-aid emergency!

11 In the Infirmary, the snot sea cucumber said her name was Slippy. Peso put her into a tray of water.

"Well done, Peso," said Shellington. "Snot sea cucumbers need water to breathe."

12 Peso tried to bandage Slippy up, but she was too slimy!

Suddenly, Slippy went shooting out of the tray of water!

13

"Flappity flippers! Where are you, Slippy?" called Peso.

"Jumpin' jellyfish!" said Shellington. "We must put her back in the water so she can breathe!"

14

"Attention all Octonauts," announced Captain Barnacles. "Injured snot sea cucumber on the loose. Let's find and protect her!"

15

Kwazii saw Slippy crawling towards the Octo-Chute, but she slid out of his grasp.

"The only way to save Slippy is by flooding the Octopod!" said Captain Barnacles. "Five, four, three, two, one …"

16

The Octonauts put on their helmets and opened the hatches. The Octopod filled with water and fish.

Slippy was still missing but the water meant she could breathe now.

The Octonauts took a net each, ready to catch Slippy if she swam by.

"Get ready, Octonauts," said Captain Barnacles. "Slippy could slide past at any moment!"

Just then, Slippy swam over Captain Barnacles' head.

"Aha, there she is!" He caught Slippy in a net and took her back to the Infirmary.

Peso put a bandage on Slippy.

"Now let's get you back into the ocean," said Peso. "And the ocean back out of the Octopod!"

The Octonauts opened the hatches again and let Slippy, and the water, back out.

The Octopod was back to normal, apart from the seaweed left behind!

EXPLORE . RESCUE . PROTECT

"Well done Octonauts!" said Captain Barnacles. "We've fixed the Octopod's leg and saved Slippy the snot sea cucumber. Let's keep working together to **EXPLORE, RESCUE, PROTECT!**"

LET'S EXPLORE THE REEF!

The Octonauts are out looking for creatures in the coral reef.
Can you spot them all?
Colour in an Octo-Alert each time you find one!

TUNIP IS SWIMMING IN THE CORAL REEF, TOO! CAN YOU FIND HIM?

CREATURES TO SPOT:

BLUE CRAB

JELLYFISH

DOLPHIN

TURTLE

OCTOPUS

HOW MANY SMALL FISH CAN YOU SPOT?
CIRCLE THE RIGHT NUMBER: 1 2 3 4 5

Answers on page 68.

When you see these pictures in the story, say the words out loud.

PESO	SHELLINGTON	ELEPHANT SEAL	CAPTAIN BARNACLES	GUP-C	OCTO-SCOPE	OCTO-ALERT

 and were out exploring when a huge

creature crash-landed on the bottom of the seabed fast asleep!

"It's an ," explained . "He's moulting and

growing new skin. But an is supposed to moult on

the beach where it's warm. It's too cold for him here and he

might get ill." radioed through to HQ. As soon as

 heard the news he sounded the . The

 was launched with an extra-strong line to tow

the to safety. With help from the whole team,

the made it onto the Octopod – still fast asleep!

 checked the snoring patient! He was fit and well.

While the  slept the team set to work to find his beach.

"Activating ," said . For days they used the

 to search beaches looking for other Elephant Seals, but

with no luck. Then one night the  stopped snoring and

woke up! He had his new skin and was ready to play.

took him to the game pod but he was too big and rough to play

there! B^U_M^P! The Octopod shook and shuddered. Just in time,

 summoned everyone to the launch bay – with the

help of the  he had found the beach. The

was sad to leave but delighted to race to the beach

to play with the other Elephant Seals! B^U_M^P! B^U_M^P! B^U_M^P!

EXPLORE, RESCUE, PROTECT!

Octonauts, let's do this! A pink blobfish is in trouble and needs the Octonauts' help.

It looks like this:  Can you find the blobfish?

WHICH CREATURE HAS SHARP PINCERS?

There are 3 spookfish hiding too!
Shout out **'EXPLORE, RESCUE, PROTECT'** when you spot each one!
Then colour in the Octonauts as they dive into action.

OCTO-FACT : SPOOKFISH
Spookfish have googly eyes and see-through heads!

OCTONAUTS, LET'S DO THIS!

Captain Barnacles has sounded the Octo-Alert – the Octonauts need to go!
But first the crew must find their gear. Can you follow the lines to help them?

SHIVER ME WHISKERS!

Daredevil Kwazii is off on a mission to explore the twilight zone. Colour in the picture to send him on his way. Add some sea creatures, too!

JUMPIN' JELLYFISH!

Shellington has spotted some interesting creatures in this tide pool! Can you help him count them? Write the numbers in the boxes below.

Starfish ◯ Hermit crab ◯ Anemone ◯

NOW PRACTICE WRITING SHELLINGTON'S NAME:

Shellington

Answers on page 68.

FISH CLOSE-UPS

Kwazii is peeping though his spyglass.
He can see lots of colourful fish!
Draw lines to match the fish to their close-ups.

Answers on page 68.

A WHICH FISH IS ORANGE?

B WHICH FISH HAS LOTS OF SPIKES?

CUTTLEFISH

PUFFER FISH

HUMUHUMU

PARROT FISH

1

2

3

4

"Reporting for training!" said Peso.

Peso was going on an important training mission to the midnight zone – all by himself!

"Do you remember the plan?" asked Captain Barnacles.

"Yep, I pilot the GUP-E to the midnight zone," said Peso. "Then after I land on the seabed, I come back as fast as I can!"

"But watch out for the vampire squid!" warned Kwazii. "He has a cape covered in spikes and squirts horrible slime. He lives in the deepest, darkest part of the Midnight Zone ..."

Peso felt a bit scared. But he knew he had to go to the midnight zone on his own, so he could help creatures whenever, wherever!

5

Peso steered the GUP-E down to the midnight zone.

"Ooh, it's getting dark, Captain," Peso said into his radio. "And I'm not even close to the bottom!"

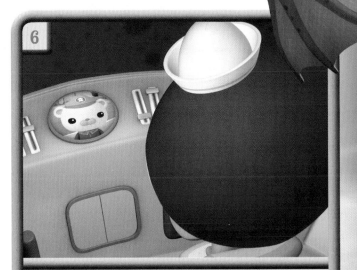

6

Captain Barnacles appeared on Peso's TV screen.

"You're doing great, Peso!" he said. "Just keep those flippers steady on the controls!"

7

When Peso reached the deepest part of the midnight zone, he landed with a BUMP.

"All right, time to go back up …" Peso said to himself.

8

"Oooh!" Peso heard a scary moan and saw glowing eyes. "I'm hurt and no one cares!" a mysterious creature said.

"I care," said Peso, fighting his fear. "Let me call the Octopod. Then I'll help you!"

"Peso to Octopod ... A creature in the midnight zone needs help, over!"

Peso didn't know what the creature was, but he had to help him!

Peso swam back to the creature.

"You won't hurt me will you?" whispered the creature.

"No. A medic helps any creature who is hurt, no matter what!" said Peso.

Up in the Octopod, Captain Barnacles couldn't reach Peso on the radio.

"He might need our help. Kwazii, **SOUND THE OCTO-ALERT!** You're going down to the midnight zone!"

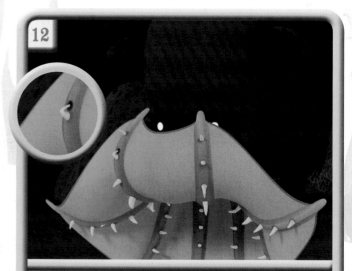

Meanwhile, Peso had found what was hurting the creature. One of its spikes was red and sore.

"I'll be gentle," said Peso, taking out a pair of tweezers.

13

Just then, a jet of bubbles gushed through the water. Kwazii had arrived in the GUP-B!

"Peso!" Kwazii shouted, loudly. "I'm here to help!"

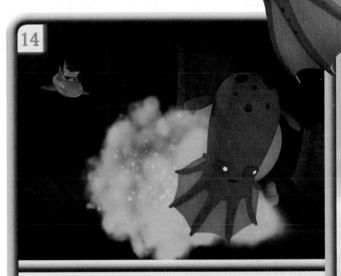

14

The creature got such a shock that it squirted green slime all over Peso!

"Flappity flippers! We scared him away! Come back!" Peso called after the creature. But it swam off as fast it could.

15

"I think I was just slimed by a vampire squid!" Peso told Kwazii.

"I'll get that monster!" said Kwazii.

"No!" said Peso. "Follow me and please be quiet."

16

Meanwhile, Captain Barnacles couldn't get in touch with Kwazii or Peso.

"Right, I'm going down! Tweak, get the GUP-D ready. Midnight zone, here I come!"

Meanwhile, the poor vampire squid was still crying out in pain. "Owwwweeee!"

"Don't be afraid," said Peso, swimming over to the squid. "No surprises this time, I promise."

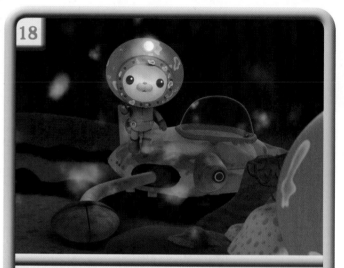

But suddenly, another burst of bubbles whooshed through the water. This time, it was Captain Barnacles!

The vampire squid was very shocked and squirted more slime over the Octonauts!

"No, please don't swim away, little squid … it's just me," Peso said, gently.

This time the squid stayed still and let Peso help him. Before he knew it, his spikes were as good as new!

"You fixed it!" said the vampire squid, happily.

Captain Barnacles and Kwazii swam over to say hello to Peso's new friend.

EXPLORE . RESCUE . PROTECT

21

When it was time to go, the vampire squid waved goodbye to his new friends.

"Goodbye, Octonauts! Thanks for everything!" he said.

"Just doing my job!" smiled Peso. "A medic helps any creature ... even if it does mean getting slimed!"

MAKE YOUR OWN GUP-A
LET'S DO THIS!

YOU WILL NEED:

- Balloon
- Newspaper, cut or torn into small pieces
- Glue (flour and water mixed)
- Craft knife (or sharp scissors)
- Masking tape
- 2 milk bottle tops
- Aluminum foil
- 2 yoghurt pots
- Egg box
- Paint
- PVA glue
- Card

01

⭐ Blow up a balloon.

⭐ Cover the balloon in several layers of newspaper dipped in glue.

⭐ Leave to dry overnight.

02

⭐ When the gup is hard when tapped, ask an adult to pop the balloon with a pin.

⭐ Ask an adult to cut out the windscreen.

⭐ Cover the gup in more layers of newspaper and glue, wrapping round all the cut edges to make them smooth.

03

★ When it's dry, use masking tape and then more layers of newspaper and glue to add all the accessories:

PORT HOLES – the bottom of small yoghurt pots

EYES – milk bottle tops

FINS – pieces of card with tabs at the bottom

MOUTH – alumimum foil rolled up and shaped

BASE SUPPORT – 4 compartments of an egg box to keep the GUP-A standing up

Instead of this stage, you could just paint the features on!

04

★ When it's dry, paint all over.

05

★ To finish, paint the GUP-A with a layer of PVA glue. This will make it shiny and strong.

EXPLORE . RESCUE . PROTECT

KELP FOREST RESCUE

Jumpin' jellyfish! GUP-E is trapped in a thick tangle of kelp. Show Captain Barnacles the way through the kelp forest to rescue Peso. **LET'S DO THIS!**

OCTO-FACT: KELP FORESTS

Kelp forests are home to kelp fish, shovel-nosed guitar fish and swell sharks to name just a few.

HOW MANY KELP FISH CAN YOU SEE?

Answers on page 68.

43

When you see these pictures in the story, say the words out loud.

| CAPTAIN BARNACLES | GUP-E | PESO | LARGE HERMIT CRAB | TWEAK | SMALL HERMIT CRAB | OCTO-ALERT |

 and some of the team had got into trouble on a beach

visit. They were stranded in a tide pool and were stuck there

until the tide came in! Back at HQ, was left in charge.

He heard the noise of a sea creature in trouble.

 sounded the , got into the

and set out on a rescue mission. Soon he found an unhappy

. He was stuck in his shell and couldn't get out.

 tried to pull but nothing worked. called

on to help. was just about to cut the

shell off when a asked them to stop. He needed a

new shell and this one looked perfect for him.  and

 explained that they borrow shells to live in. When

they grow bigger they have to find a new shell home. Perhaps

 would know how to get the shell off without breaking

it! radioed through to the Octonauts in the tide

pool. told how to carry out a crabectomy.

THE HERMIT CRABS

 put a hose into the 's shell and then he pumped

5 times **5 4 3 2 1** and whoosh the flew out of the shell!

The was delighted to be able to move into the pink shell.

But the was left with no home. Just in time,

and the team got back with a beautiful new

shell. It was just right for the  !

FLAPPITY FLIPPERS!

Peso needs to help a hurt lemon shark! Follow the line with your finger answering the questions along the way.

B WHICH GUP DOES PESO DRIVE?

A NAME 2 THINGS PESO KEEPS IN HIS MEDICAL KIT.

C NAME PESO'S LITTLE BROTHER

D WHAT MUSICAL INSTRUMENT DOES PESO PLAY?

Answers on pag

GUP MATCH

Can you draw lines to match the gups to their shadows?

GUP-A

①

GUP-B

②

GUP-C

③

GUP-D

④

GUP-E

⑤

Answers on page 68.

OCTOPOD HEADQUARTERS

The Octopod HQ is where Captain Barnacles and his team track weather patterns and plan missions.

Colour in the Octonauts before they dive into action to help an injured sea creature. What creature do you think is on the Octo-Screen?. **DRAW IT!**

B

HOW MANY
OCTONAUTS
CAN YOU
COUNT?

C

CAN YOU
CIRCLE THE
SMALLEST
OCTONAUT?

Answers on page 68.

1

"Dashi to the Octopod! I'm about to take some pictures of the coral reef."

Dashi was on an important mission to record life in the coral reef.

2

"Very good Dashi!" said Captain Barnacles.

Dashi swam over to take a picture of a colourful fish.

3

But as Dashi looked through her camera to take a photo, a small creature peeked out from behind a rock.

4

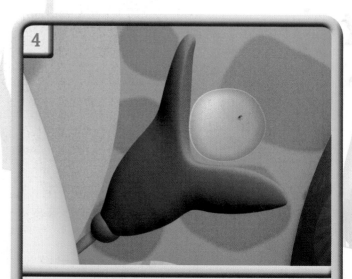

A bubble came out of its claw and ...
BOOM!

"Woah! Oh help!" Dashi went spiralling down to the seabed!

5

"Yikes!" worried Peso. "What's happened?"

"Dashi come in," said Captain Barnacles. "Octopod to Dashi."

But there was no answer from the brave Octonaut.

6

"**SOUND THE OCTO-ALERT!**" said Captain Barnacles. "We've lost contact with Dashi and we're going after her."

The crew rushed to the launch bay and jumped into GUP-A.

7

8

9

"It must be a giant shrimp monster with huge BOOMING claws!" Kwazii said to Peso. Peso imagined a big, scary shrimp monster. He gulped.

10

"Octonauts, our mission is to find out whatever made the loud noise that knocked out Dashi," said Barnacles. "Ear protectors on."

11

12

13

Kwazii pounced to Peso's rescue.

"I'm OK," said Peso. "There was a loud boom!"

"Don't worry, me hearty, I'll get you back to GUP-A!" said Kwazii.

14

Back at GUP-A, Kwazii called Captain Barnacles to tell him about Peso.

"No sign of the monster here," said Captain Barnacles. "I'll come back. Barnacles out!"

15

Captain Barnacles was on his way back to the gup when he thought he saw the monster. His ear protectors fell off as he moved forwards to investigate … **BOOM!**

16

The Octonauts on GUP-A heard the loud noise. And then they saw Captain Barnacles' ear protectors float past!

"Yeow!" said Kwazii. "Cap's in trouble! Let's go!"

The crew reached the captain just as he was waking up on the seabed.

"I'm off to find this monster!" said Kwazii. He swam towards the booming noise.

Brave Kwazii saw the claw of the monster. Then Peso quickly wrapped up the claw in one of his bandages.

Captain Barnacles picked up the small shrimp - it wasn't a giant monster at all!

"I'm a snapping shrimp," said the little sea creature. "I snap my claws when I'm frightened. I thought you wanted to eat me!"

"But how can a wee creature be so noisy?" asked Kwazii.

Dashi had an idea. She could use her camera to video the shrimp snapping his claws!

EXPLORE . RESCUE . PROTECT

Back on board the Octopod, the crew watched Dashi's video of the tiny shrimp.

"Aha!" said Captain Barnacles. "The claw makes a bubble! And the bubble popping is what makes the **BOOM!**"

The tiny shrimp was very small but very noisy!

"Another successful mission, team! Now let's rescue some more sea creatures – **OCTONAUTS, LET'S DO THIS!**"

CREATE YOUR OWN OCTONAUTS MISSION!

Have a go at making your own Octonauts and sea creatures out of children's modelling clay. Use clay rather than dough, as dough will go soft in water. Shape the clay into a ball for the heads and roll into sausage shapes for the arms. To make the eyes and mouths simply press a pencil point into the clay. Fill a large bowl with water and now you're ready to act out underwater rescue missions!

01 Sound the Octo-Alert, a storm is on its way! Use a straw to blow up a storm in the bowl of water.

OCTO-FACT: STORMS
If a storm is big above water, it'll be just as big below the water.

02 A turtle is stuck in a whirlpool made by the storm! Kwazii is coming to rescue him. Tie some string around Kwazii and hold on tight to him. Swim him into the bowl of water to save the turtle!

03 Kwazii's rescued the turtle! Hurrah!

Now make up your own underwater adventures! You could make a reef lobster with sharp claws, or an octopus - don't forget to make all 8 arms!

OCTO-FACT:CURRENTS
A current is like a river in the ocean that's always moving.

GARDEN SPOT

These pictures of the garden pod look the same, but 5 things are different in picture 2. Can you spot them all? Colour in a number each time you find one.

1 2 3 4 5

WHO LIVES IN THE SUNLIGHT ZONE?

The sunlight zone is near the surface of the sea. It is bathed in sunlight during the day and is where most sea creatures live. Here are some creatures that live there. Point to your favourite!

BLUE WHALE

HABITAT: The Indian and Pacific Oceans
FOOD: Tiny floating plants and animals
OCTO-FACT: It is the biggest animal alive on earth!

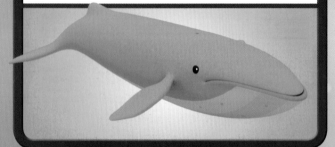

LEMON SHARK

HABITAT: They live in tropical waters
FOOD: Fish
OCTO-FACT: It has special electric sensors on its nose that help it sense if food is near!

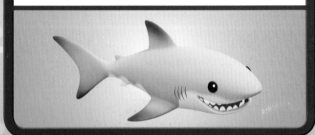

JELLYFISH

HABITAT: Found in every ocean
FOOD: Small fish
OCTO-FACT: Its tentacles sting. They can be as long as three school buses!

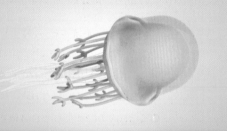

ORCA

HABITAT: Found in all oceans
FOOD: Fish, squid and even small whales
OCTO-FACT: It swims and hunts in groups called pods – sometimes the pods have as many as 40 orcas!

LEATHERBACK SEA TURTLE

HABITAT: Found across the globe
FOOD: Algae, seaweed, jellyfish and squid
OCTO-FACT: It is the fastest moving reptile in the world and travels further than any other turtle.

AGGREGATE ANEMONE

HABITAT: Rocky, tide swept shores along the Pacific coast of North America

FOOD: Algae, fish and tiny floating plants and animals

OCTO-FACT: It makes copies of itself by splitting down the middle, until one anemone becomes two, and so on and so on … until there's a whole group!

OCTOPUS

HABITAT: Many regions of the ocean, especially coral reefs

FOOD: Clams, crabs and even other octopuses

OCTO-FACT: When it's scared, it can shoot out ink or change its colour to disguise itself as a rock!

DECORATOR CRAB

HABITAT: Rocky, tidal areas of the coasts of Australia and the United States

FOOD: Algae and tiny creatures in or on the sea floor

OCTO-FACT: It gathers shells, algae and anything it can find, and sticks them to its shell to hide from sharks!

REEF LOBSTER

HABITAT: Rocky ocean bottoms in tropical parts of the world and Japanese waters

FOOD: Clams, crabs and fish

OCTO-FACT: To survive undersea storms, reef lobsters crawl in large groups to deeper water. This is a 'lobster march'.

PORCUPINE PUFFER

HABITAT: Mostly found in tropical waters

FOOD: Clams, crabs and tiny creatures

OCTO-FACT: It can suck water into its huge stomach, and blow up its body like a balloon to scare away other fish!

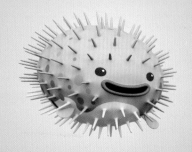

WHO LIVES IN THE TWILIGHT ZONE?

The twilight zone is deep under the sea. It is the lowest part of the ocean that the sunlight can reach. There are some creatures down there that want to meet you!

GIANT SQUID

HABITAT: Found in all the world's oceans
FOOD: Fish and other squid
OCTO-FACT: Has the largest eyes of any animal!

GIANT SPIDER CRAB

HABITAT: Mostly found off the southern coasts of the Japanese island of Honshū
FOOD: Algae, crabs and fish
OCTO-FACT: It can stand as tall as 2 grown-ups and can live up to 100 years!

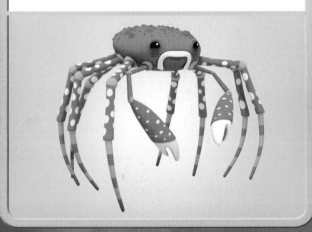

COOKIECUTTER SHARK

HABITAT: Warm, oceanic waters worldwide, particularly near islands
FOOD: Fish, squid and whale blubber
OCTO-FACT: It will bite through anything – even submarines – and eats its own teeth!

BLOBFISH

HABITAT: Deep waters off the coasts of mainland Australia and Tasmania
FOOD: Anything small and edible that floats by!
OCTO-FACT: It has such weak muscles that it doesn't swim. It floats and waits for food to arrive!

WHO LIVES IN THE MIDNIGHT ZONE?

The midnight zone is the darkest place in the sea. It's a place so deep that the sun can't shine there. Meet the creatures who live in the dark. Point to the one you like the most!

VAMPIRE SQUID

HABITAT: Around 600-900 metres under the sea, where there is no sunlight
FOOD: Jellyfish, shrimp and squid
OCTO-FACT: It can shoot green slime!

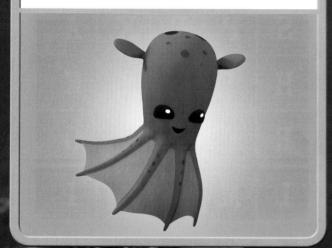

SLIME EEL

HABITAT: In cold water in burrows on the sea floor, as deep as 1200 metres
FOOD: Tiny creatures on the seabed
OCTO-FACT: When it's scared, it squirts out a thick slime!

ANGLER FISH

HABITAT: Mostly in open water, but it sometimes lives in the deep sea as a bottom dweller
FOOD: Fish, squid and tiny creatures on the seabed
OCTO-FACT: It uses its light to attract fish – and then it eats them!

VENT FISH

HABITAT: It lives near hydrothermal vents – cracks in the ocean floor which let in heat from the earth's core and warm up the sea.
FOOD: Crabs and molluscs
OCTO-FACT: A slow swimmer who likes to be alone!

OCTONAUT SEARCH

Can you find the Octonauts' names in the word grid? They can read from left to right, or top to bottom. Tick the names as you find them.

BARNACLES ☐ TUNIP ☐ DASHI ☐

SHELLINGTON ☐ INKLING ☐ TWEAK ☐

KWAZII ☐ PESO ☐

B	A	W	O	F	T	S	P	E	K	A
Z	I	E	D	A	S	H	I	C	W	K
C	G	H	L	N	O	E	P	L	A	G
E	R	N	S	O	P	L	M	O	Z	I
B	A	R	N	A	C	L	E	S	I	H
A	T	S	U	W	E	I	T	C	I	D
E	U	F	R	A	K	N	G	T	E	S
I	N	K	L	I	N	G	U	W	A	Z
N	I	B	A	R	S	T	S	E	H	I
A	P	E	S	O	P	O	R	A	N	S
C	O	L	E	S	E	N	A	K	L	D

Answers on page 68.

GOODBYE, OCTONAUTS!

Your final mission is to colour in Captain Barnacles, Peso and Kwazii as they dive into action in the GUP-A.

ANSWERS

page 7 KWAZII'S TREASURE MAPS
There are 6 maps hidden through the annual.
They are on pages 15, 22, 31, 48, 51 and 67.

pages 22–23 LET'S EXPLORE THE REEF!
There are 3 small fish.

pages 28–29 EXPLORE, RESCUE, PROTECT!
The crab has sharp pincers.

page 30 OCTONAUTS, LET'S DO THIS!
Kwazii – spyglass
Barnacles – binoculars
Peso – medical kit

page 32 JUMPIN' JELLYFISH!
Starfish – 3
Hermit crabs – 4
Anemones – 5

page 33 FISH CLOSE-UPS
Cuttlefish – 3
Puffer Fish – 4
Humuhumu – 2
Parrot Fish – 1
A – Cuttlefish   B – Puffer Fish

pages 42–43 KELP FOREST RESCUE
Path A leads Captain Barnacles through the Kelp
Forest to Dashi and Shellington.
There are 6 kelp fish.

page 48 FLAPPITY FLIPPERS!
A – Bandages, stethoscope, medical manual
B – GUP-A   C – Pinto   D – Xylophone

page 49 GUP MATCH
GUP-A – 3   GUP-B – 1   GUP-C – 5
GUP-D – 2   GUP-E – 4

pages 50–51 OCTOPOD HEADQUARTERS
A – The kelp cake is behind Tweak.
B – There are 6 Octonauts.
C – Tunip is the smallest Octonaut.

pages 60–61 GARDEN SPOT

pages 66 OCTONAUT SEARCH

B	A	W	O	F	T	S	P	E	K	A
Z	I	E	D	A	S	H	I	C	W	K
C	G	H	L	N	O	E	P	L	A	G
E	R	N	S	O	P	L	M	O	Z	I
B	A	R	N	A	C	L	E	S	H	H
A	T	S	U	W	E	I	T	C	I	D
E	U	F	R	A	K	N	G	T	E	S
I	N	K	L	I	N	G	U	W	A	Z
N	I	B	A	R	S	T	S	E	H	I
A	P	E	S	O	P	O	R	A	N	S
C	O	L	E	S	E	N	A	K	L	D